W9-AQQ-483

THE ABC BOOK

By Steve Foxe

A GOLDEN BOOK • NEW YORK

© 2020 The Pokémon Company International. © 1995–2020 Nintendo / Creatures Inc. / GAME FREAK inc. TM, ®, and character names are trademarks of Nintendo. Published in the United States by Golden Books, an imprint of Random House Children's Books, a division of Penguin Random House LLC, 1745 Broadway, New York, NY 10019, and in Canada by Penguin Random House Canada Limited, Toronto. Golden Books, A Golden Book, A Little Golden Book, the G colophon, and the distinctive gold spine are registered trademarks of Penguin Random House LLC.
rhcbooks.com
Educators and librarians, for a variety of teaching tools, visit us at RHTeachersLibrarians.com
ISBN 978-1-9848-4927-4
Printed in the United States of America
1 0 9 8 7 6 5

DID YOU KNOW?

There is at least one Pokémon for each letter of the alphabet. Here are some of the ones you'll see from **A to Z**!

Aa

ALCREMIE attacks with **aromatic** creams!

Bb

BULBASAUR loves to **bask** in the sunlight.

Cc

In Kanto, you have the **chance** to meet Bulbasaur, **CHARMANDER**, or Squirtle early in your travels.

Dd

DREDNAW defends itself with massive jaws and a **dense** shell.

Ee

EEVEE is known to **evolve** into **eight** different Pokémon!

Ff

FLABÉBÉ and its evolutions, **FLOETTE** and **FLORGES**, are never **far from flowers**.

Gg

When the air **goes** cold, **GENGAR** is close!

Hh

HO-OH brings **happiness** to anyone who **holds** one of its feathers.

Ii

IGGLYBUFF is still learning to sing. **It is** one of the most adorable Pokémon **in** the world!

If **JIGGLYPUFF** sings its song like a lullaby, you'll be asleep in **just** a few minutes!

Jj

KOMALA keeps a close hold on its log, but it has been **known** to cling to the arms of **kindly** Trainers, too.

Ll

LATIAS can reflect **light** to alter how it **looks**.
It **loves** to fly side by side with **LATIOS**, which can project images
into someone else's mind. And there's nothing more relaxing than
a **laid-back** ferry ride on a **LAPRAS**!

Mm

MEOWTH simply **must** collect any shiny objects it finds!

MIMIKYU **masks** its true appearance to get closer to Trainers and other Pokémon.

Nn

NINETALES is **native** to the Kanto region.

Now it can be found in a different form in Alola, too!

Oo

ODDISH plants its feet in the soil in **order** to draw nutrients from the ground.

Pp

PIKACHU is a **Pokémon** that stores electricity in its cheek **pouches.**

PSYDUCK'S mysterious **power** gives it **paralyzing** headaches!

Rather than chase its prey **quickly**, **QUAGSIRE** is known to wait with its mouth open for food to enter by accident.

Qq

Rr

According to legend, **REGIGIGAS** built **REGISTEEL**, **REGICE**, and **REGIROCK** to be smaller models of itself out of magma, ice, and **rock**.

SNORLAX sleeps most of the day. When it's not **sleeping**, it's probably eating!

Ss

Tt

TOGEDEMARU'S spiny fur **typically** lies flat, but it stands up straight when the Pokémon is **threatened**!

Uu

Not much has been **uncovered** about **UNOWN**, but researchers know this **unusual** Pokémon is shaped like ancient writing.

Vv

VULPIX **varies** between regions. In Alola, it has adapted to **very** cold weather. In other known regions, its body burns with a **vibrant** flame.

Ww

A **wealth** of Pokémon **wander** beneath the **water**. Can you spot **WAILMER**, **WAILORD**, **WOOPER**, and **WISHIWASHI**?

What about **WOOLOO**,
way up above?

Xx

When seen from far away, **XERNEAS** looks like a giant **X**. Legend says it can share everlasting life.

Yy

YAMPER yearns to scamper after people and Pokémon, and has a lovely **yellow** tail.

Zz

ZACIAN and **ZAMAZENTA** **zig** and **zag** through the Galar region, inspiring myths and legends.

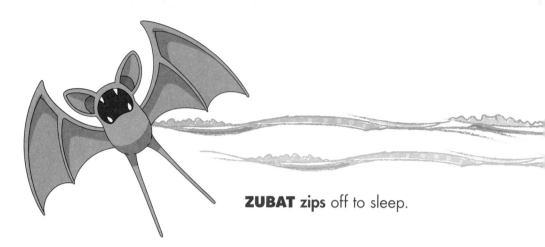

ZUBAT zips off to sleep.

Now go to bed and catch some **Z**s!